he Hole in

MW00716297

Written by Lynn Nicol • Illustrated by Don Sullivan

Mouse went in the hole.

Squirrel went in the hole.

Rabbit went in the hole.

Raccoon went in the hole.

Owl went in the hole.

Porcupine went in the hole.

Ouch!

Let's get out!